T0353861

Amor perfeito

ANY SIMILARITY WITH REALITY IS PURE COINCIDENCE

Isabel Helena de Brito Manique

AuthorHouse™ UK
1663 Liberty Drive
Bloomington, IN 47403 USA
www.authorhouse.co.uk
UK TFN: 0800 0148641 (Toll Free inside the UK)
UK Local: 02036 956322 (+44 20 3695 6322 from outside the UK)

This book is printed on acid-free paper.

ISBN: 979-8-8230-8968-5 (sc)
ISBN: 979-8-8230-8970-8 (hc)
ISBN: 979-8-8230-8969-2 (e)

Library of Congress Control Number: 2024918668

Print information available on the last page.

Published by AuthorHouse 09/02/2024

authorHOUSE®

CONTENTS

"Pansy", "viola" and "violet", in Portuguese amor perfeito.

"Plants considered to be "pansies" are classified in Viola sect. *Melanium*, and have four petals pointing upwards (the two side petals point upwards), and only one pointing down, whereas those considered to be "violets" are classified in Viola sect. Viola, and have two petals pointing up and three pointing down.

Most modern "pansies" (possess) "a well-defined "blotch" or "eye" in the middle of the flower.

The name "pansy" is derived from the French word pensée, "thought", and was imported into Late Middle English as a name of Viola in the mid-15th century, as the flower was regarded as a symbol of remembrance. The name «love in idleness» implied the image of a lover who has little or no other employment than to think of his beloved.

The name "heart's-ease" came from St. Euphrasia, whose name in Greek signifies cheerfulness of mind. The woman, who refused marriage and took the veil, was considered a pattern of humility, hence the name "humble violet".

In Scandinavia, Scotland, and Germany, the pansy is known as the "stepmother" flower; an aitiological tale about a selfish stepmother is told to children while the teller plucks off corresponding parts of the blossom. The German name is *Stiefmütterchen* (lit. ‹little stepmother›); in the German version of the tale, the lower petal represents the stepmother, the large upper petals represent her daughters, and the small upper petals represent her stepdaughters. The Czech name for the flower, *maceška*, also means "little stepmother" and is said to derive from the flower's resemblance of an evil woman's sullen face. In Slovenian, the flower is instead identified with an orphan.

In Italy, the pansy is known as *flammola* (little flame).

In Israel, the pansy is called *Amnon Ve'Tamar,* (ותמר אמנון), named after the rape story of Amnon and Tamar, in which Amnon raped his half-sister Tamar.

In Hamlet, Ophelia distributes flowers with the remark, *"There's pansies, that's for thoughts"* (IV.5)."

Wikipedia

My name is Violeta. These are my memories. I owe my name to my beautiful, scintillant eyes, musk green with a shadow of violet: miracle eyes. Eyes which have witnessed miracles. Eyes which existence is a miracle.

Who is going to tell him? I have been recently told by specialized doctors, following an impromptus and very unexpected urgent hospitalization, that I have maximum one year to live. My body is damaged, giving up on me.

My visceral self has turned violet, all of it, all organs damaged, ailing in pain. The pain is unbearable. I am Violet(a).

My soul is fresh and young, though. I keep a candle burning and pray often that I survive and live long, very long. Would like to hold my grandchildren in my arms, see them laughing, dancing, loving, learning.

I do have a perfect, clear mind: my IQ is a perfect score. Extremely rare, if not at all unique. What does not ease my pain.

I hope. Always hope; I am the eternal optimistic.

This book is dedicated to love.

'L'amour a un caractère si particulier, qu'on ne peut le cacher où il est,

ni le feindre où il n'est pas.'
Marquise de Sablé

MY DADDY

The attic was cold, dusty, smelled like fungus were growing in the corners of the tiles in the roof. A shed of light shinned from the roof, warm, leaving a ray of sun in the floor.

I had been punished. My dad was in a bad drunk mood, again. He came home early morning, from the cafe in the nearby village. He often would throw anything he would find around at me when he arrived in the early hours of the morning.

My dad was the town's mayor. Thin, tall, grey. Respected. People around would fear him and collude with him. I would not say they worshiped him, but he was liked by many. He was a provider, the godfather of most of the village.

During the Summer, almost every weekend there was a marriage, mostly of immigrants who returned home from France for the season. He was the *padrinho*. The godfather. From hundreds.

Never locked his car in the village, would leave his car with the windows open. Who could ever steal from him?

He dined with the police chief and treated the police agents as family. An example, a paradigm to follow. The mayor that year after year governed the town.

Every Sunday, the sacred day in which is only possible to work till noon, he would take his family on a tour of the high mountains walling the valley. One day the light brown van had its breaks malfunctioning. We descended the perilous and serpentinuous small roads without breaks.

Now, when I sit writing these intimate words, I vividly recall the brown Toyota van, a family car for a family man.

I have good memories of my childhood and adolescence. I may be wishing to forget what I am not able to remember. Not everything is worth remembering.

It was dark outside. So early still. My mother came and awoke me up, gently placing her wrinkled hand on my shoulder. The bed was warm, the blankets smelled fresh, and I did not want to awake up. *Violeta,* she called softly, *it is time, we need to go now.*

THE FARM

The days we would go to the farm started in the very early hours of the morning. Often at 4 a.m. we would stand up, get dressed in the dim light of the moon, the clothes prepared the evening before, sitting in the chair next to the bed. There was a feltro smoking pink panther on the wall. The height was that of a little girl, of an 8 or 9 years-old girl. The pink panther had a black tall hat, and its protruding eyes followed you overall in the room. The background was kiwi green. I adore green.

We lived in a small once prominent house. A small castle in my eyes. A traditional white Portuguese farm house that had housed generations before us.

Years later, had wool sweaters in that exact same shade of green. My grandmother used to say that the world is full of small stars that shine through together. All is interconnected.

That morning we went once again to the farm. I really enjoyed it. There was a grey house, not painted, still the cement bricks. There were fruit trees in the internal pateo.

Years later, the complex reminded me of a Mexican hacienda. The things a person remembers later in life. The pateo had apple trees randomly distributed.

That Saturday we left to the farm at 4 a.m. and a bit. Descending the stairs of the apartment to the red van parked just in front of the apartment, I was 6.

My baggy clothes were from my cousin who was a bit older. Were warm and suitable to work in the farm, not new but all holes had been mended by my maternal grandmother who raised me for the most.

I was wearing the shawl my mother knitted, dark green and warm. My hands were swollen by the cold, wounds in my fingers.

The early mornings, sunrise's can be so cold. The cold impregnates one's bones. I curled myself in the back seat of the van and dormitated with the familiar voices.

Invariably my mother and father would be going to the farm.

Invariably also, we had workers coming with us. They came from the villages around. Appointments were made a few days before and there they were, awaiting outside the house to be picked up when the only light in the street was a lantern's dim light.

There were a few workers that were assiduous to come to work at the farm. Almost always the workers were men. Dressed in dark clothes, often cladded with a hat.

The workers would board the white van, occupying the back seats. It became a ritual, so unchanged it was. The radio played folklore intervalled by the hourly news. By five thirty or six in the morning, we would have arrived at the farm.

My mother would prepare a large breakfast, cold, for everyone. Coffee and wine would be served alike. One of the workers would gather wood outside for the fireplace and we would all eat at the kitchen table. The kitchen was simple, modestly furbished.

The furniture was used, but served its purpose well. There was a little square table in the mid of the kitchen, with 4 banks. The table was brown with a stripped pattern. There was running water, only cold.

If we wished to wash the dishes with warm water, we would boil it in the old cooking pan at the fireplace. In the iron pot.

After, the workers would start the day, by then around seven o'clock. I would be called to look at a bird's nest nestled in the rose tree. Or a cricket would be imprisoned in a matches' box, singing the beautiful melody crickets do.

When the first cherries decorated the cherry trees, I would be summoned to try the first cherries. Once in a while, a work for the labor class in school would make me sit in the stairs to the attic and sew for instance a pillow with a Sarah Kay doll.

The stairs on the side of the house led to the attic. There, on top of cartons, we could spread the apples and pears destined to the household's consumption. We would sporadically remove the rotten apples and pears, salvaging any piece of fruit still suitable for consumption.

Upstairs, there was also a sofa, dark green and run down, yet very comfy. We could nap there after lunch or during the afternoon hours.

If tired in the early hours of the morning, we could also nap there. There were windows but no glass in the windows. There was an old door only. It was a quite place, almost religious, to rest and unwind.

To the other side of the pateo there was a long one storage piece. Straw bales were kept there, on the second floor. There were water snakes that would hide between the bales. The straw was used to bed the pigs, chickens, and rabbits on the other farm.

Tractors and other farming utensils were kept downstairs. Large doors opened from the structure to the outside.

Outside, across the small farm road there was a tank, to wash clothes and gather irrigation water, and an olive tree. Not far there was a mimosa tree, when blossomed smelled so nice!

SO MUCH SAVING AND NOW I'M LEFT WITH NOTHING

It was as every Sunday. We went somewhere. An extensive family, local. We went to visit my baptism godparents. I would not be able to drive myself, but my dad would always drive. Always the same way, the same trees, olive trees.

Small, whitewashed houses. I always loved small houses. I am a procrastinator, with a slight streak of compulsiveness, like cleanliness. Small houses are easier to clean. Often plastic curtains. Long plastic fils.

I enjoyed the trip, would seat in the back seat of my dad's van. My dad always had red cars.

This Sunday we drove again slowly. A sinuous road. I dreamt of one day living in such a little house. I wanted to be primary or secondary school teacher.

We arrived. Their dog barked as always. The dog would never enter the house, my godfather was a hunter, like my dad. They hunted foxes. They hunted rabbits, and hares. We would feast on the preys. Stews with tomato sauce, cabbage and lots of spices and aromatic herbs.

We arrived. It was just past 10 a.m., my godfather run to open the gate, stilling the dog. It was a sunny day, it is so often sunny in Portugal. The air was clear and the sky bright blue.

I liked my godparents. They were kind to me. As always, we entered the ground floor and the fireplace was churning away with burning wood. It smelled home. Nothing compares to a fireplace on Summer, warm, warm.

We helped finish the preparations for the lunch. As always I set up the table. We had paper napkins, a small luxury in the days. We often had paper napkins when the family came together. Still now I collect beautiful paper napkins, the nostalgia of missing home. I collect napkins depicting birds, flowers, small children, beauty. English porcelain, anthracite grey last century drawings imprinted. A couple of lovers in the woods, she seating on a granite stone under a tree.

My dad drove hallucinating fast down the mountain, warning that the breaks did not work. I hide behind his seat praying that we would survive the descent. It was a spacious old van. Used often for transporting the relatives to the market from the farms were they inhabited.

THE MOUNTAINS

These were high mountains. There are perineal pines spread all over, with little shepherds houses dotting the view.

Granite is the favorite source material for building. The van accelerated in the descent and then would turn in the curves just at the last minute. Hallucinating.

Miraculously we would be every time closer home. Unsure how it happened, but eventually we arrived to the foot of the mountain. The air was fresh, my nostrils hurt with every exhalation.

What I remember most vividly are the pine tree brunches brushing against the windows of the van as we passed driving without breaks.

It were two houses in a row. My granny's was the second, counting from the parfumed mimosa. I adored the flowers and the scent. The flowers would soon fall into the ground making it a yellow sheet of small parfumed balls.

There was a pig pen next to the mimosa. There were years in which porks were lodged there, some other years cows or other cattle, like sheep. To the left, another compartment stored grains for the Winter.

There was a compartment against the wall as we entered. Covered by a wooden plank. I recall my aunt bending over that container and picking up the grains to feed the animals. Poultry was also raised, chickens, turkeys, cocks.

I took delight in the familiar scents: the grains, the mimosa, my aunts long hair tied up smelling like blue soap. Much smelled like blue soap, including clothes. It was the soap of choice.

Every Tuesday the ambulant merchant would arrive. His van was a paradise of colours for a child: he opened his stand and in the shelves there were all types of boxes in all types of shapes.

The attic let rests of light in. There was dust everywhere. A small wooden table, with a small platform to place hot coals, reddish orange and hot. My mom had placed an old black and yellow cover on the table. It always reminded me of honey, of bees.

I had been punished. I must have been 4 or 5 years-old and it was not always clear to me what punishments were. Of what I was being punished for. Why. I was trembling and crying. Sad. Feeling scared and lonely.

There was little to play with in that attic.

Some stored empty wooden boxes. A light brown suitcase, empty, waiting to be filled when of the next trip.

We did not travel often, nor long. Yet, every year we would go to Algarve in the Summer. There, we would eat fatty, sugary Berlin balls filled with cream. And yoghurts, lemon, coconut and ananas.

Why had I been locked in the attic this time? Seemingly I broke the small chair. Do not recall having broken anything. Things would appear broken and invariably the finger was pointed to me.

Often I had no clue what they meant. My mom would turn a blind eye and a sewing supplies' small basket was thrown at me, or I would be pushed to the ground. The basket was full: needles with wedged thread, one crochet needle protruding from a pink crochet ball. I, instinticvely moved in front of my mom who stood up behind the table during the argument, and bent when the basket approached. Missed me narrowly.

My dad was so often drunk, this was not an uncommon event. So many tears, so much despair, so much verbal violence.

Often, it was said at the meals that the downstairs neighbours had argued loudly during the night and that he hit her. I could only think I had not heard anything. Except our own arguments and shouts.

One could never be sure *how we had him*, how my dad was that night. The café was a few hundred meters away…. And he visited that cafe so very often.

A second skin, to be drunk.

From the moment that the 8 o'clock night journal had finished on TV, silence started installing itself. We would seat around the table, me, my mom and the elderly neighbor across the patio.

We would just had to wave from our own kitchen window, she would nod affirmatively and some ten minutes later there she was, seating also around our round kitchen table. Tia Mariana.

We played cards and she taught me to bluff. She was from a small village away in the mountains and would search the rivers for mineral semi-precious stones. Semi-precious gems.

She would bring her stones which we would proudly display in our closet. Shinning, purple, grey and anthracite.

She would also bring us samples of tissues we would make sacs for beans and cereals.

DOMESTIC FAIRY

My mom was a domestic fairy, the sewing machine was easy for her. All the while we awaited my dad. Tia Mariana was normally gone by the time he would arrive, I suspect he timed it. He knew she was no longer there.

There were very few hematomas to attest to his bad temper. The pain could be excruciating, and yet very few hematomas.

Now looking back, after so many years, I do not see the innocence I then saw in it. I would imagine him unhappy because of lack of professional advancement and an unhappy marriage.

Now I would imagine what I at once point called *domestic prostitution*. I know. It is denigrating and likely unfair. Too hard. But then I was younger and more critical.

Now looking back I see lies and pretense.

So little likely was what seemed to be.

But back then the aim nwas to survive another day.

And another and another.

I can't be sure. My mom would give me *Nestum* of rice or chocolate almost every morning, almost every breakfast. Her face said that likely there were drugs on it. What I call forgetting drugs. I just recall what could be misplaced intimacy.

At a very small age. Being sold off to my dad's friends. To my dad's partners. To my dad's clients.

A pink panther my size then, must have been about 1 meter high, smoking. On a bright green background. On the wall of my room. The room I shared with my sister.

I had this orange blanket, which I would place on top of one bed and unroll till the other bed, covering the gap between the beds. It would be my own tent, my own place there under, a place only mine. Where nobody from the family was welcome.

Once in a while a sound, a smell, a sound make me nervous beyond explaining. Not sure why.

I recall the nauseating smell.

The being treated as second best, without a reason to be second best. My mom saying that when I was born, nuns were then the nurses assisting births, the nun had turned me upside down, hit my back, but I had not cried.

Lack of oxygen in the brain they said. They said I would be *slow*. Seemed true when she would say it. Now, I recall her saying it to the extended family, maybe more often than needed.

Just like my dad would place my right hand between his hands and pretend to hit it…. He really hit it. It would hurt.

The daddy, he would say, he loved his family so much he would say. He is dead now. And I make a conscious effort to uphold and preserve his memory.

But…. I do have my moments.

ANOTHER WEEKEND

Often marriages in the weekend. Looked like my dad was the godfather from most in the town and surrounding villages.

Often Portuguese immigrants living in France, working in a factory, as hairdressers, mechanics.

I would often buy new socks, or a new undershirt, or a new shirt from my dad on the weekly market.

Would have saved the money from working cleaning for my aunts and friends of my mom. My aunts would give me a little money sometimes, my godparents every time they saw me, on a white envelope.

Tra-la-la…. la-la-la…., there I was jumping instead of walking or running. The street had the traditional Portuguese stones. Irregular: *little horse, little horse.*

It was my First Communion. My little white dress was embroidered with red and pink flowers, the green leaves perfectly embroidered.

MY FIRST COMMUNION'S PHOTO

My First Communion's photo has my face scratched off, a white stain result of scratching the black and white photo with a sharp nail.

My sister grew up deeply jealous of me.

For a Catholic family, events as a baptism, First Communion, Profession of Faith, marriage are all very special. My dress was pale blue, with blue embroidered ribbons flanking my chest, overlapping my shoulders and upper arms.

On my chest violet flowers and bright green leaves, embroidered by me.

I wore long knitted white socks. And black ballerina shoes. Short, boyish haircut. A smile as wide as my face. And musk violet scintillant eyes.

My grandmother, fully dressed in black, with a stole above her head and a black cape was standing next to me.

My grandmother was blond to her death, even when the silver shade had conquered her hair. Bright blue eyes denounced some Jewish blood on her veins. Long gone, distant genealogy, still visible.

My cousin, Eduardo, next to me. We were the same height, same complexion, same weight. Same age almost. Could be confounded from a distance, wouldn't it be for the manner I was cladded.

My mom and dad are also in the photo, which was taken in the village's church main altar. Gold columns, Baroque style ornament the Virgin Mary at the centre of the altar, behind us.

It's a beautiful, cheerful photo. Except that my face has been scratched off by a person's nail.

It was a day of celebration, after the mass, my Communion shared with others the same age and their families, we had a superb meal. A feast.

Then, we danced to the sound of my godfather's accordion. He learned to play during his military service in one of the Portuguese firmer colonies, Angola.

My godfather truly loved my godmother: he would say that he loved her more than she loved him, so immense was his affection towards her. And then would tell her that every time she descended the stairs outside their house, his heart would pound *bong, bong, bong*. He died years later of brain cancer. A swift death.

I had a secret little crash on my handsome cousin, Eduardo. His older sister was also present, her and his boyfriend João. Much later, his older sister, Adelaide, broke up with João because he was caught smoking a cigarette.

I have happy memories of my First Communion day!

YEARS LATER I GOT MARRIED AND BECAME A MOM

Years later I got married and became a mom. My daughter was born on the warmest day since 1964. The sun soared burning high in the sky.

I do not want to have my daughter going through what I do not remember but was quite sure had happened. The fear. The anxiety. The unconscious cry that something definitely wrong was looming to happen.

My condition was always perilous, now that I look back. I would brave into new countries, meeting new faces and places. And yet…. There was always something dark that I could not put my finger on.

I saw it in the way people treated me… it wasn't suspicion or a schizophrenic mistrust of strangers. I was treated like worn clothes, like second hand clothes. No matter what. No matter the effort to please.

I became shy. Bookish. Distant.

My marriage happened in October, 13th October to be exact. A sunny warm day. Live music playing, many dancing. Joyful cherishing of us.

My bridal dress was light pink decorated with pearls. To this day I collect pearls. Broken white, eggs' white pearls.

YOU ARE ALWAYS DRUNK, I SAID

My father teared…. Whether these were fake tears or real tears, can't say. When I recall the event, my opinion about it changes depending whether I am having a good or a bad day.

He got upset. Stepped into his chestnut coloured large van and drove away. I run after him and could step into the back seat. Sat tight and held my breath.

Once again… he was drunk. Was difficult to know if he was ever sober… at least, sober enough.

I was crying. Scared. Frightened that we would have an accident. My heart was pounding, I thought everyone could listen to it. My hand palms felt humid and cold.

I was shivering. I leaned forward in the seat behind the driver's seat: *Father can I do something for you?…* I was crying and kept repeating *I am so sorry…. I am so sorry… I did not mean it.* I might have meant that he was always drunk, because he was.

What I did not mean was the result…. I had half consciousness that he may be using my words and twisting them to serve him… to make me feel bad. To make me feel guilty. To humiliate me.

The van would drive fast and slow down… like a dry cough of a sick moribund. I did contemplate death there and then. Could be we would have an accident. I hugged him behind his seat, hugging the seat head rest.

Not sure how long it all lasted. I still have the trauma of driver's who take both hands away of the steering wheel whilst driving. My dad did it often. Mischievous, to put it mildly.

That night, pitch dark outside, the would take both hands off the wheel, lean to his right, to the passenger seat next to him and then lean back into his seat.

Was a small man, if now I think about it. His violent outburst and continuous menacing demeanour made him a giant at my eyes then.

Of course it's many years ago. We passed near the hospital's entrance, facing the priest's house. Then my primary school and from there down the hill. Then he turned right. We were going home, finally.

The little chapel with its clean pergola and pulpit stayed behind us.

He was calmer now. I thought he could fall asleep, after all the outburst emotions explosion of before. The farm and our house was nearing and finally we arrived near the large house we called ours. He stopped and I went out.

My mother, who had been all the time in the passenger seat, looked at me disapprovingly. She often looked at me disapprovingly when my father was stoned drunk as that day.

He would throw things at her if she colluded with me. My sisters would be either out clubbing, in the town's main café with friends and acquaintances or simply in bed. I always felt sorry for my mom.

I knew what punishment was.

To be locked in a closet for days shivering. Looking through the room through the keyhole.

I know how to be silent and often my shoes last decades. The soles are barely worn: I have learnt to levitate and not to touch the floor. Better said, not to step into the hard floor. Like a ballerina.

A souvenir from my infancy and adolescence: not to make noise, like a mice.

Not to wear the soles of shoes which may not be replaced often.

I do not blame my mom. Often I would hug her and think to myself how could she cope and survive. Years later, I realised that unwittingly, or consciously, not sure which, it was a dance between both. A collusion. She availed his behaviour and he felt empowered by her avail.

She could control me and let people abuse me… because otherwise my dad would have left us both, us and my siblings.

Now looking back, and me being so religious as I am, my heart and conscious forbids me from speaking evil of the deceased…. Just. I now think she might have wanted it that way.

A photo comes to mind: her, her friend, my aunt and my godmother. On the top of the stairs… my mom with her arm around the shoulders of my aunt.

Yes.

REVENGE

What is strikingly are my mom's eyes and facial expression: revenge. Revindication. I knew she had spoken about my abuse to them... they all knew, except maybe her friend and this is a big maybe.

I took that photo. Many years ago. The blossomed purpure red roses on the bottom left corner, giant in comparison with the 4 on the top. The brown tiles in the background, some broken beige corners contrasting with the dark brown. The dark brown of catholic monks in a monastery.

Mine is a story greater, so much greater than myself.

I have a very high IQ. And, my intuition serving me, I can be in more than one place at once. Not always, and not in my imagination only.

I do have a fertile imagination. Yet, I can really be in two or even three places at once. Depends on my health and how well do I feel that day.

I have day dreams and night dreams. Greyish. Multiple shades of anthracite grey.

Of course, I am infatuated with myself, and I am a narcissist. Otherwise I could not have survived then and could not cope now.

I am kind, but rational. My life revolves about me, myself, I and mine. Mine are my family, friends and acquaintances. Those I care enough about, to care.

For a person transcending space and time.... For whom Einstein's Theory of Relativity is a reality, pettiness and small mindedness is hard to cope with.

The dichotomy of being really intelligent and yet, for those I grew up with be little more, if anything more than old clothes. I have been called *second-hand clothing*.

I am second-hand clothes.

Being the most intelligent person in the room, by all tokens, and yet. Being everyone's slave.

They abused me and one can use one's imagination of the most terrible deeds and yet I guarantee will fall short of reality.

Punishments involved spanking with a man's leather belts. Near the entrance of my parents' room, the bed to the left and the closet with the centre mirror piece to the left.

In Portugal women (and some men) use slippers. Spanking with a skipper.

Years later, the ubiquitous Brazilian soaps over lunch and in the evening on TV.

Slave Isaura.

Black woman with the used slipper.

The black one with the cracked cap said my cousin laughing at the dinner me and my husband were so kindly invited to, whilst visiting back close family.

Mine is a terrible story, because of lasting so long and being so horrible: so horrible as to giving me sleeping pills smashed in a cup of milk.

Or of Nestum, honey oak-type of meal given to children.

And then putting a tube similar to a lab Bunsen-burner and incinerating my visceral self. I awake and with every breath I take via my mouth, every word I say, I smell burnt flesh.

Freaking really, if it's one's internal organs flesh letting that smell. Fetid. Disgusting. Revolting. Nauseating. Very worrisome, very difficult to stay calm and continue breathing.

Breath, learn to breath says the lady in the blog. She intends it well. My breathing analysis stating, in a graph, that I am constantly in state of alert, in a flee-ready stress stage, even if I am seating down and should be calm. The sensors were applied and I was left alone in the room.

Who is hurting you?

I do have a fertile imagination.

Why is it important for me to write all this? I would not wish my worst enemy what my darkest hours were.

Complots and ops.

I am money, due to my high rationality, high intelligence and clear mind.

Often people say *now is clear,* after I explain. I have been victim of deep abuses of many sorts, so yes I am money. I am exploitable. Sellable. Can be trafficked in a normal labour, working and family settings.

Who can blame my exploiters? It's all so long ago, and yet so present.

Social media.

The elusive passerby that mumbles a word.

The direct insult.

Never meant anything bad with it, of course.

Psychologists and psychiatrists have attested to my mental sanity. I did doubt that I could be schizophrenic, that I was seeing bad where good was meant.

My mom's *you always see the worst in everything.*

MY MOM

Recently, I saw the photo of an old colleague, now a lovely acquaintance. I could hear the voices that she gave cyanide to her mom. The photo was to celebrate the passing away anniversary of her mom.

Cyanide to her own mom.

I thought about my own mom. Never meant her any harm and would never hurt her. Have never hurt her. Did all I could during her long disease to help her and soften her pain.

How can someone do what my acquaintance did to a mother?

These memoires are very difficult to write.

The ghost of my shadow, even in nebulous and dark days. Can't shed it away. Can't get rid of it, so I hope that writing about it will put the demons to rest. And avoid the demons to watch it being done to others and do not intervene.

Here is my story, thus.

Hoping that others will have the signals and signs recognised and a kind hand will help.

Often was said of me *it's too late, the abuse was too long and too deep*. It's never too late,

I pray. As long as one lives, one is alive. So, I continue my narrative. My aim is that with understanding, kindness may arise.

Often I hear the *I did not know that*. So now you know.

Nobody should have had to go through what I went through, and often still go through.

Moreover so, because was inflicted on me from the day of my birth, hours after my first cry of coming to the world.

Religion did play a role on my inflictions, what did not, and does not, stop from being firmly religious.

Abuse at so tender age, for 13 years, involving being caged, internally incinerated like a pig, bled like a swine, and burnt, stabbed and amputated….Etc…

Never goes away. The scars are visible physically. And people do not forget. I am now middle-aged.

And some people still remind me, viciously, maliciously and often, remind me of what I recall wishing I could forget. Remind me daily. Of the anthracite grey half memories. Of the intuitive remembrance. Even when one is as sick as I am… many do not let down.

However, kindness exists too: this book is to the kind. As my thank you.

MY BIRTHDAY PARTY

I loved the way the sun shinned through the 'persianas': the air was always warm and fresh. I used to awake up early. Some days, the days we went to the other farm, the one with the fruit trees, I was awaken between 4 a.m. and 4:30 a.m.

In the dawn hours, there were all sorts of noises: the cows of the neighbour, the birds, the chicken and the swine. Welcoming, sonorous, comforting.

A bright new day, full of opportunity.

Today was my birthday.

My room had closets with prominent pieces in velvet. Dark red wine velvet. A mirror in the closet in front of the bed.

A large bed. On the wall to the left of the window me and one of the neighbour's daughters had made a flying kit, in rose papier-mâché. Five corners. My friend, Maria, painted beautifully.

Cinq. Someone recently whispered that word when I was crossing the road just outside of Galleries Lafayette in Paris. Five corners.

Maria had drawn and painted with watercolours a Walt Disney's Minnie. The Minnie had a ribbon in white with red balls. A fuchsia dress and high heel shoes. Her right leg semi-curved. I saw a similar pose last year in social media, my acquaintance and her husband next to her turning his back to the camera.

Is it all connected or is it me? Perhaps I think too much and link too many dots.

I did try to fly that kit, but not in a beach or in the mountains. Just outside the house. It flew, turning in curves in the sky. It twinned against the bright blue sky, pink and blue.

The neighbour's house ten or so meters away, the blinders were almost always closed. One could never be sure who was looking.

It is still so, one can never be sure who is watching oneself.

Anyway.

It was my birthday and I was turning thirteen. A knock on the door of my room. My mom. No *happy birthday* wishes. In all honesty, I never celebrated my birthday.

MY BEDROOM

That was the room I was sleeping in, and yet the house had several stories, floors, many rooms, several bathrooms and kitchens. And, the floor we occupied only had four bedrooms with four beds and we were with six: my parents, my three sisters, and me.

That was not my bedroom. It was the bedroom I occupied. My eldest sister was away to study at university in England. This was her bedroom.

I did not have a bedroom in my parents' very large manor house.

As often, when amidst us, *la petite famille*, I did not have a seat at the eating table. The table in the kitchen was in wood conglomerate, white bordered by an aluminium bar. The seats were caramel brown. Six seats.

And, nonetheless, often there was no place for me. I served the eaters. The diners.

Waited till everyone dined, in my lent bedroom. Read often: devoured books. Unconsciously to put my mind off things, I now realise. But also because I simply adore to read. Freud, Dostoyevsky, Miguel de Allend, Camões and Fernando Pessoa.

Eating every three days someone told many years later. See, I am quite sure this story is not an untold story. I am the conversation in the pauses from work, the gossip of the town and elsewhere.

I often feel undressed by people's eyes. Really have the impression many have seen me naked, at least in a metaphoric sense.

I am just so damn smart. Tell me…. Can you teleport to other existential planes? Seemingly I can. Arguably. Are semi-memories, remembrances of what I can't forget. I wish I could forget what I do not remember.

Back to my birthday party: there was none. I never have had my birthday celebrated till I was away to study in college.

Somehow the parties did not happen. Not sure why. Money maybe. Why would those who saw me as a *hand broom* spend any money on me?

Yes, I can clean beautifully and fast. Adore to see cleanliness around me, even if, admittedly, now I am somewhat lazy when it comes to cleaning. I am getting old.

My boss, one of my bosses, there has been a string of very admirable and valuable bosses in this career of mine. My boss said *you have to be careful, you are getting old*. I think he meant old as in wise, because in reality I look younger than I am. Not sure why would one needs to be careful to be wise.

As you can read, I doubt often and I am not sure of most. Helps me to be highly intuitive, identifying danger omnisciently and esoterically.

My birthday parties were on my head: in my head, in my books and whilst doing house chores or working in garden and in the farm my mind would often fly away. Still does. I try to be present and listen to my interlocutors.

I often succeed at listening.

And I often succeed at disconnecting,

I can be surrounded by talking and noise and we remain at noise. I have absolutely no clue of what was said: this is a skill I perfected with time.

Because I listen so well, took me a long time to learn to shut my ears when some I dislike, or and do not find worthy of being heard, talks.

I love people. Just some people are so mean to me that if I am to be happy and optimistic, I do not listen. At all. What, for those who perceive my not listening, somehow infuriates them, and they start shouting.

The dining table at home was, by rule-of-thumb, as loud as a market place. They speak so loud really. I often speak softly, sometimes whisper. If I am loud is because of an important deal or event for work; in business I can have a higher intonation than privately.

My birthday parties in my head were so much fun! I had an extensive family. Many aunts, uncles, cousins of several degrees (first, second, third, ….). Not sure they were all family except the ones who were often at the parties.

Because me not having birthday parties did not mean we were party less. No. There were parties often, marriages almost every weekend.

My dad was really the godfather of most in town and villages around. And I did like my extended family: they would come to my imaginary birthday parties.

I also find animals are family. The animals, and we invariably had chicken and swine and pigeons and rabbits.

They came to my imaginary parties. We would all sing, play the accordion (this was my baptism's godfather skilled playing of the accordion) and dance.

I was part of a youth folkloric dance in Portugal and could really dance the 'fandango'.

In my imaginary birthdays I received presents! Clothes, so beautiful clothes.

I love beauty. In all forms.

Jewels, real and fantasy: I always received jewels in my imaginary birthday parties. We had flowers in the jars in the large table. Long table that was, in my imagination.

Invariably the imaginary birthday parties took place outdoors. In the sun, fresh air and wonderful smell of the flowers in the garden.

I have been fortunate and happy to be so spoiled and loved in my imaginary birthday parties.

BAKING CAKES

I do not remember, I swear I do not. But the side conversations, the rumours, the malice in my mom's hairdresser had it that I stole fruit from my uncles' farms when I visited and offered to help in the garden. I do not think I did.

Do not recall, not even in my anthracite grey existence and experiences.

I believe, and not sure I should or not believe this, that I am innocent. I do not rob. I am not a criminal and strive to always do the right thing, also in law matters.

Maybe there were strawberries missing and it was easy to blame me.

I will later in this story tell you that my mom suspected me, accused me really of stealing 200 escudos at my 16 years-old.

And I had to leave. To not let people in the town talk more than they may be doing then, I went to study in another place. Far. I went to suburbs Lisbon. Because of being the thief.

To this day, and I swear to God, risking not to go to heaven when I die, that I have no clue which 200 escudos was she talking about. She put them under the mattress of her bed. And then did not find them back.

The cleaning ladies, plural, were there often, several times per week. The door of the house was seldom closed, even not closed sometimes when we went on an outing. But it had to be.

Can't recall; might be the price for being in several times at once if one really wishes to. Can one really remember all those different existential planes differences? Likely not.

I can't prove I did not steal and I think my mom could not prove I stole.

I left the house. Could still return for some weekends, if I ironed and cleaned and helped. Nonetheless, no longer officially lived there.

One of the ironies of my life was that I baked so many cakes for others. A tradition, actually only my mom and aunts had the tradition to my knowledge: if we were to visit an aunt, we were to back a cake.

Cinnamon cake.

We did have an electrical mixer, mind you, my parents actually had luxury and a lot of electrical utensils, immigrants coming from France or business clients and acquaintances of my dad.

We had some of the last novelties, even an automatic photographic camera in which the photos were printed immediately. At the time was fancy.

For a growing up girl denied, for the rare exceptions, a place at the eating table, to be the one to bake the cakes was demoniac.

Pardon my honesty. Smelling the ingredients, mixing them till a smooth pasta. Buttering the form and bringing the whole to the electric oven.

MY PARCEL OF LAND

At the corner of the garden there was an olive tree. Its spine bent, like an old lady overlooking the sight of the valley. I come from the fruit valley. Mostly cherry trees, which the legend has were planted by a king to his Scandinavian princess who missed the snow of home.

The valley parfum is delicious. In any season. Spring is the most perfumed, with the blossomed cherry trees' white petals dancing in the breeze. Feels magic. A safe haven on earth.

The dark secret the town hides is not apparent. Because my abuse was perpetrated and enforced by so many in that town and vicinity villages.

There is a movie *The secret in their eyes* whose title matches the secrets in the eyes of those surrounding me when I grew up.

I pretended not to see. Like a procrastinator who lets time pass before an exam, refusing to study hard, idle and feeling guilty for procrastinating.

The fear of failing and the fear of succeeding.

The fear of a briefly worn dress that one wears with so much style and pride, just to be taken away after a few hours of wear. Giving it to an acquaintance of my mom.

Not being able to hold property, not even a key in the lent bedroom's door keyhole.

My dad's *You don't mind, do you?*…. actually, I mind and do not want to give my temporary, lent possessions. Nothing. They gave nothing, and still give not much, if anything.

Becomes an habit, the abuse.

I have been terrified all my life about becoming habituated to abuse, because if one can't change it, the survival instinct is to bend. And bend and keep bending.

Until bending is the automatic, irrational reaction to any situation.

The empowerment courses later in life do not help that much, do they?

Anyway.

Please do not take it away, I would whisper. My smoked dress with spaghetti bands. I adored it. D. Rosa was our seamstress, incredible but true: most of my clothes were tailor made, in my early years.

Later in life I dressed, and very much behaved, like a boy. Short hair, whiskies even if faint, the clothes of my male cousin. To protect me, my very religious mom would say.

A while ago, in a business trip my boss said, to a colleague, on me *your friend is a drink'* And yes, a drink I have been for so long: a beautiful piece of clothing,

I could wear it once or a few times. Not long. Then, without notice would disappear from my lent's bedroom closet.

I had to ask for it, or say I had been looking for it. Did not always received a reply, other than the normal slap or beating. Till I asked no more. I would then see my clothes on someone else.

My body shorts light green and brown, flowers and leaves. My sister descends the outside stairs and seats in the fence to the garden wearing my clothes, but does not say anything on it.

Not an apology of *oh, I wore your clothes because are nice* or *sorry, did not have the opportunity to ask you whether I could wear these*, and *is it okay for you?* No. Looking away from me, avoiding eye contact. A malicious grin on her face.

Perpetuating what everyone did anyway.

It's a strange existence, mine. Not meaning to blame anyone.

Maybe I caused it myself. Or at least caused parts of it. And yet I was abused at the age of 1 day for the first time.

Like a doll. Very strange that the first word my daughter said was just that: *doll*. They touch you, do unspeakable, unfathomable things to you. And keep on doing.

My mom later lied that I did not breath when being born. I was a still birth.

I was brought up to the world by nuns. Back then the nuns were the nurses on the hospital of the town, which then was a village. Only became a town later.

From little I was special, specially if one believes in ghosts and the esoteric world.

My mom would often go to witches, truthtellers, shamans who would heal broken bones, urticaria, skin rashes and much more. Would fix matrimonial issues with the burning of herbs and praying to saints. Depending on the ailment, so the Saint would be chosen.

I tried to retain the best of each experience: when a small child is abused daily and even several times a day, one is constantly in guard.

Always scared.

Takes the back seat in class at school so one can see the others. Never turns a back to an open door. Takes one's overcoat with one to the place one is in. One's school sac is full of other days 'stuff'.

The pencils are used to a few centimetres, till the moment the fingers can no longer hold them.

They did not ask, just took without asking and did not replace what they took. If one asks about it, they spank oneself or accused me of not believing in the goodness of people.

In the end, I had been uncareful and left the coat somewhere unattended, this is why it disappeared. Not always so directly put, yet omni presently put.

Life becomes full of secret messages and codes in words, colours, behaviours. As a child I would in the street jump as a pony, again and again, for hundreds of meters.

Looking back at it, it was my scream for help. I was being abused.

Then, one day much later I have been given a backpack from a Portuguese brand then called *Cavalito*. It disappeared.

One day I had it in the apartment. Then it was gone. I had two options: *giving* it voluntarily what meant not asking about it when it was gone. And *letting it be gone* voluntarily by not being too sad and too disappointed when it was gone.

Like a model modelling clothes and shoes and bags to customers.

In due honesty this is why I am writing this: not revenge. Not coming to terms with it. I pray for others. Love children and really hope from all my heart no child ever endures what I endured.

I am allergic to cheese. Because was closed for two weeks in a small cheese curing chamber my parents held. I was cleaning it. They said the door closed from the outside and they could not find me.

This is me: my phobias, my fears, my hesitations, my ambitions and hopes.

PEAS, BEANS, ONIONS AND GARLIC

We would grow an array of vegetables and fruit. Peas, beans, onions, garlic, cabbage. Parsley and other aromatic herbs.

We used awnings to gather the harvest. We made braids like those made with horses tails' hairs, and women's long hair, to tie the garlic together.

People would work in the farm, casual workers. I also have worked much in the farm. From little. That day was a late September afternoon. I was picking up the beans and bring the full buckets to the awnings.

The small blue car stopped abruptly near us and a second degree cousin came out. Looking at my mom, who was seating in a chair threshing the beans he said crying: *my father-in-law has passed away.*

My mom's face became white. A death, natural or not, with us was not a mere death. I believe my mom was scared of retaliation for the sins she had committed on me. For what she had done.

The village on itself was a nest of rats really: they would keep the silence amongst them, protecting each other fiercely. But on that beautiful valley, tourism slowly flourished.

It is so beautiful there. And one never knows what a tourist might come to know. My mom treated death as a threat. Same for my dad and siblings. Not that otherwise they felt remorse or even cared that much for what they did to me.

But not having the benefits of the abuse or if someone from outside discovered, this could be an issue.

Child abuse is something ambivalent: the victim is not really a victim in the *strictus sensus* of the word. A victim is normally pardoned easier, pampered, comforted.

From child abuse people keep a distance and often take advantage of it to their own benefit, as long as people do not see it as taking advantage of a disadvantaged.

It already happened, if we could have done something we would have had... we did not know. Now that is done.... A pity really... she is lost. 'What a shame, so much potential.

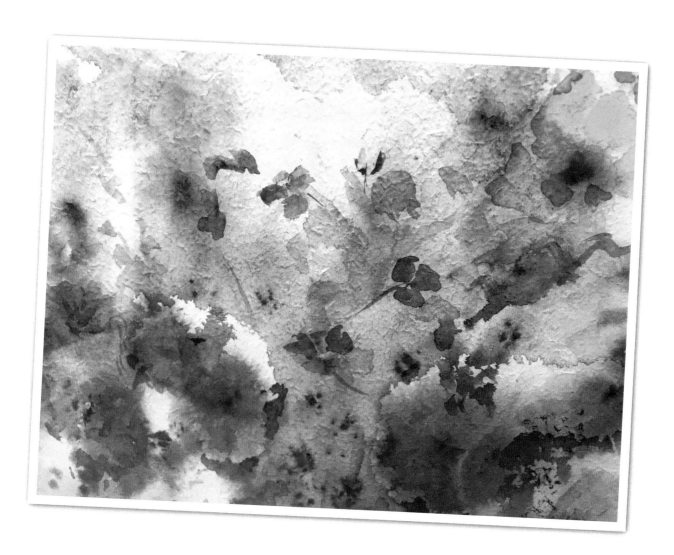

MY REAL PARENTS

In my head I came to realise I could choose other parents. Only did it after my mom passed away. I came to choose JFK and Marylin Monroe.

In my head I became the out-of-wedlock daughter of love and passion: I am, in my head, Marylin Monroe's daughter.

Still love my other mom of course, just that being Marylin's daughter makes it more bearable the insults I have been inflicted. Because before becoming Marylin's daughter I often wondered which mother would have watched and done nothing, this is the mild version, better colluded and inflicted what she inflicted in me.

She wanted the favours, sexual and others, of my dad. And maybe of others. Achieved them by using me, giving me as the bargaining chip. Like in poker. In my mind I became a Kennedy.

In my mind I have been engaged, or married, not sure which, to Barack Obama. He calls me Isa and I call him Bobo, in my mind.

Of course all in my mind. I am a Kennedy-Monroe Obama. My surname. My family name.

Helps me cope. All delusions of a lonely mother.

I am a very proud mom myself.

I WAS JUST SIXTEEN

Hello girl! How are you? my cousin Joaquim salutes me. He was seating in his veranda with his wife. In the sunny afternoons, many seat next to the doors and in the verandas in Portugal.

I walked a lot. I was walking back from the town. On my right hand, holding a yellow plastic bag with fruit. My backpack with my school books balanced as I lifted my left hand to salute my cousin.

I walked a few more meters before stopping near the swing. The swing was made of metal painted beige. The seat was embraced in Baroque style. I seated on it and begun to move slowly: forward and back, forward and back.

I sang and my notes echoed in the wind. Was a warm sunny day. The slight breeze gently fustigated my face and brought my hair in disarray. I had shoulder length hair.

Still now love longer hair…. It's important for me.

My grandmother had very long, past her knees silver hair: thick, shinny, still with golden reflexes matching her blue eyes. I visited her so often as I could. Dreamt of living in her house for years, still in my bucket list to buy it and restore it one day (soon).

I started ascending the stairs, leaving behind the swing. Because the entire swing was made of metal, it made this cracking noise. Like wood being cracked, with each swinging movement.

The higher I went in the swing, the higher, acuter the noise was. In the open air, the noise turned heads: the elderly neighbour and his donkey, Joana, turned their heads. In the distance I could perceive his smile.

His wife, also called Joana, came and brought him a glass of fresh water from the tank. Potable I expected, yet maybe not so healthy. She turned her back and walked to their small, one story house near the road.

He called 'Joana!'. She turned to him, and asked what she often asked: *You call me or the donkey*? He did not reply. His deafness was legendary. Continued ploughing the soil with his donkey in the punishing son.

I started ascending the stairs. The stairs were made of light grey marble intertwined with grey and violet ascents. Slightly cracked by the passage of the years.

The fence was also in iron. Coming to the veranda my mom received me with a grin: where is the money? I had absolutely no clue what she was referring to.

The 200 escudos you took.

I didn't take any money.

I entered the house and she followed me closely. Maybe I had wandered in my sleep, sleep walking, and really taken the money.

The nagging doubt.

I sometimes could see shadows, smoked figures, details not nitid. Felt a hand caressing my hair. A presence mostly. I doubted whether it was a real being. Still do. And yet....

Have felt it so long that became common place. Came to accept it. Not really long for it, because it are ghosts. But in some strange way their presence comforts me.

What for so long scared me, with time became comforting and a companion in the lonely and crowded moments.

The shadow presence, and presences at times, never hurt me: it is a hug, a caress of my hair, a kiss on my cheek, a caress of my broken foot.

My mom passed in front of me and showed me the made-up bed, lifting the bottom right corner of the mattress as she mumbled *where is the money, what have you done with it?*

I could perceive the light blue blanket and the blanket and cover. There was nothing there but the wooden sticks supporting the mattress.

In the evening, my mom told my dad about the missing money. No. I had not taken it I guess. But can't be sure. Can't remember ever taking it. And yet was my own mom accusing me of it.

Why was she so sure it had been me? There was no doubt in her voice or manner: I was being convicted without the possibility of defending myself.

If I had taken the money, where was it? I went to my small bridal box, a small trinket in dark varnished wood near the bed. It wasn't there. Maybe under my pillow? It wasn't there either.

A DAY AT MY GODPARENTS

My godparents lived in Coimbra. We would visit with Christmas, Easter and some of the main holidays.

Coimbra is Portugal's university town. When I was growing up, my godfather, Toto for António, reminded me of a Roman, imponent to small me.

We passed the Roman aqueduct in the distance. We stop in one of the many ancient squares to drink. And then we drove further.

My godparents were still young. They had three children, two girls and a boy. Adelaide was five, Joaquim seven, and Rodrigo was ten.

Their house was a perfectly squared pale yellow house. The dog, Bobby, would keep guard in the patio. There were laces in the downstairs door. We seldom went upstairs, the visits were received in the pale blue tiled kitchen downstairs. The TV was always on. My favourite programme was *MacGyver* and it was going to play that afternoon.

As it was customary, we gave two kisses in each other's cheeks.

How are you? So long… how long has it been? At least two months.

It was Sunday and we would miss church, the noon mass, because we went to visit my godparents.

Can we watch the twelve o'clock mass?, asked my mom. My godmother acquiesced.

The food was always partially prepared, the salad and cucumber from my godfather's little garden.

It's always so neat, everything is shining, I thought. The tiles reflected my shadow when I passed. The floor was so clean that it was possible to eat from it. This was my youngest sister's comment, each time. Every time we visited, he would state the same sentence, with the same intonation.

We sat down at the kitchen table: not different from my parents kitchen table. The women prepared the vegetables, removing the old leaves and roots. We ate a lot of vegetables. Everyone I recall always ate so many vegetables.

It's lamb in the oven, my godfather said. My grandfather, who was seating the corner of the sofa, that under the large window near the lite fireplace, smiled. His favourite dish.

Do not make so much noise, we can't hear what the priest says, said him. From the garage, separated from the kitchen by a small corridor, could be heard the laughter and strong, resonant voices of the men. My dad and my cousin, and also my godfather were playing cards.

This was our ritual: women cooked, men played cards and planned their next hunting excursion together. In different rooms. My grandfather was too old to join them.

Grandad, do not snore so loud, said shily my youngest cousin.

Not only was the house so neat, the garden was equally impressively well taken care.

PUNISHMENTS

I miss my right nipple. An open hole where it used to be. At least it's not on the side of my heart... even if a heart is somewhat in the middle of a person's chest, it points to the left.

Otherwise, every time I would think about the nipple I miss, I would cry of melancholy.

I have been caged for days without food, water thrown into the dirty floor, which to survive I licked. Dirty, sparely dressed, insects in my mouth. My eyes infected with pus. A dog or cat for sole companion.

I have been incinerated, for hours. The pain is excruciating. Very few humans could survive such torture.

I had my right hand amputated. Miraculously, I do have both hands.

Burnt alive.

Stabbed.

A flesh eating bacteria infected my right leg, upwards, inner, and a scar as large as a coin attests to this.

Scars ensued and remain. Scars of many types.

My punishers have been creative and resourceful.

THE SCAR IN MY FOREHEAD, JUST BETWEEN MY EYEBROWS

If you are so intelligent, what are you doing here?

The people around me are not supportive.

I have some catchy scars. My right ear is missing a piece, I do have a scar in my forehead, between my eyebrows. Which I keep plucked, so to distract, deviate as much as I can, attention from my large scar.

It's actually just a few centimetres. In my imagination, when growing up, everybody noticed it ew the woundfirst of anything else when looking at my face. It was made worst by the fact many stared long at me.

I can't change it, even if now is very faded away.

Officially I got this scar when falling as an infant.

Officiously I was stabbed with a knife, to deformed me. So that the public would pity me. Rumours are I run to my grandmother's house, who gave me a needle and thread and in front of a mirror I sew the wound myself.

Sew myself my wound on myself.

Red thread was all my grandmother had, the rumours ran. It must have hurt, do not remember the pain, so long ago it is.

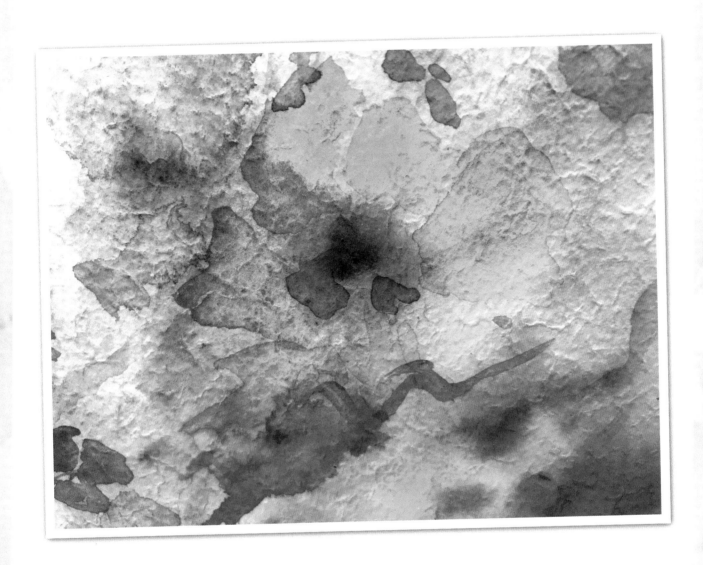

WATERMELON

I was in London, in a hotel just off Picadilly Circus. In the lift there was a small boy. Maybe 1 year, or just not. He did not say anything to me. He did not say anything to the lady who was carrying him. I assume his mother, given the resemblance.

The toddler, baby boy was wearing a sleeveless shirt with small watermelons imprinted on it. He was a chubby boy.

My uncle Luis kept me watermelons when I was growing up. We often paid them a visit in their farm and he, more often than not, had an oval large watermelon kept for me.

It always stroke me the watermelons were always large and oval. Never round.

Often mature, very often too mature, bordering spoiled. Very sugary.

It was a ritual: we parked in his and my aunt's patio. Descended the car and he would welcomed us.

Offering a glass of dark red, homemade, wine to my dad. Never white, always red.

And to my mom and me, after kissing my mom on both cheeks, would look at me and with an enigmatic smile would say *I have kept you a watermelon, only for you.* Always the same meaning, not always the same words.

Then, he would open the door of his storage room downstairs, take what to me looked like always the same knife and from one end to the other, on the largest axis, slice the large watermelon.

Like my dad, he was a recreational hunter. The shotgun above his bedroom closet, like my dad. The ammunition in the original square box, like my dad.

Same brand of ammunition like my mind. Mind us, there was only one shop in the village to buy such things.

The knife was a large bladded hunter's knife. With which he and my dad and other uncles would remove the hunted preys' scalps and fur.

Same knife used for the killing of the pigs. Every uncle and aunt I recall, and there were many, killed a pig at least once yearly. Either they would raise the swine themselves, or buy it just ready to be slaughtered.

To who never heard the screams of a dying pig, what I now will write will resound meaningless and empty: it's one of the most horrifying sounds on Earth, a pig being bled to death and slaughtered, begging to be spared.

It's a loud scream. Heard kilometres away. Especially on a valley. It is agonizing.

One wants to run and save the pig.

The pig tries to run free. And sometimes succeeds in liberating itself, at least momentarily.

Furthermore, it is a lengthy process: sounds an eternity that death. It is being bled to death, after all.

My uncle's Luis knife was the knife he took everywhere a pig was being killed. Slaughtered. I would have preferred he would have used another knife to slice my watermelon.

Because was my watermelon: I ate from it first, and sometimes ate from it only, alone. Rarely but sometimes: it was a large watermelon after all, and it was too much for me.

For some unknown reason to me, I associated and associate still watermelons, the ones purpure inside, with clean and healthy teeth.

Maybe because some of my aunts and uncles had less perfect teeth.

Perhaps because a watermelon's slice is like a mouth's smile in shape. I still think of teeth.

Maybe because the seeds are dark brown and some had a dark brownish smile.

Or because a watermelon's red flesh resembles a bleeding mouth. Blood. I am not good with blood. Its sight makes me want to throw up.

I have ambivalent feelings about watermelons. In Portugal are not really a luxury, exotic fruit, given many farmers cultivate them. Watermelons are often too sugary. Just a bit too much. Not all so healthy.

The skin of a watermelon reminds me the fur of a large cat: a puma or a tiger. The stripes.

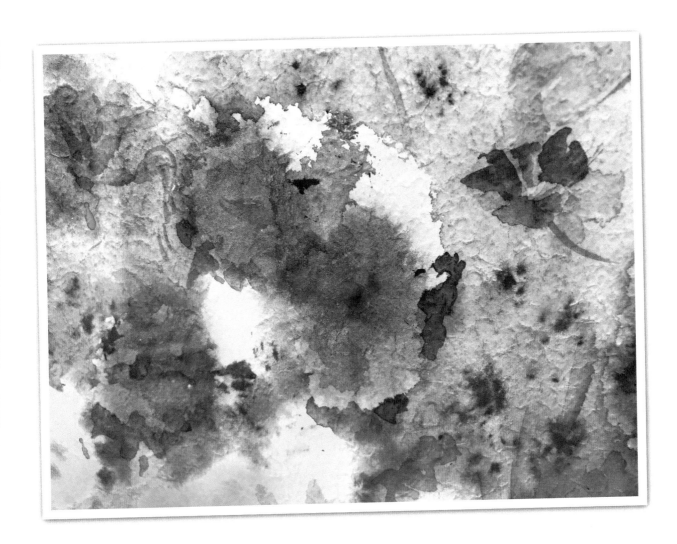

BATHING ME

The cleaning lady bathed me. Downstairs.

The tiles of the living room downstairs were identical to those of the kitchen: yellow pale with dark brown and orange flowers designed to resemble wild flowers.

I can't be sure if bathing me was the cleaning lady's payment, or tip.

She, D. Gabriela, could cut all flowers she wished to, from our garden. To bring with her to the church when she cleaned it every Thursday. To decorate the church's Virgin Mary main, and adjacent, altars.

I was a young lady, a teenager. Given the choice I would have preferred to have bathed myself.

Felt uncomfortable. Prefer not to remember it.

MY T-SHIRTS

I tend well to my assets. Inclusive my clothes.

Because anything I could keep, and was not given away, was such a rarity, I cared carefully for all I had. And have.

I am a volunteer. Anywhere I can help. Anything I can do. Anytime I can learn.

Volunteering often means small souvenirs as a token of appreciation. Small rewards. Inclusive, often, t-shirts.

I marched for humanity.

I walked for the impoverished housing.

I helped paint a local chapel.

I volunteered to a premature neo-natal hospital's ward.

I was a children's soccer team coach.

A coach for special Olympics (Paralympics) ice okey team.

Search and rescue team when someone got lost, in cooperation with the Red Cross.

Almost always I received t-shirts in exchange for my efforts.

T-shirts I cherished so much. Washed by hand with the soap meant to wash myself with.

Dried the t-shirts in the sun.

Opened them to breath in the fresh air, every now and then.

My family gave all my t-shirts away. I do not have one left. None can be replaced. They were one edition items, linked to the commemoration of an event.

I now have new t-shirts. And when I wear one of my t-shirts now, I think of the t-shirts of then. So many years have passed and I miss my t-shirts.

Worse of all, the t-shirts were given away without requesting my authorisation to do so. Likely because I very likely would have hesitated to give away my t-shirts.

Nobody asked me.

Nobody means it, of course; I do wonder *why does (nearly) everybody than does it?*

MY DARK GREEN GRADUATION DRESS WITH BRUSHSTROKES OF GOLD

I saved for the dress. A group of girls, in a girlish mood went to eat ice-cream. And do window shopping. Near the ice-cream shop there was a small boutique: self-made clothes. Two dresses were displayed in the windows' mannequins.

One dress was long: a boat décolleté, long to the feet. Was simple and sophisticated simultaneously. Painted with brushstrokes of gold.

I bought it with my savings. For my graduation.

Wore the dress proudly. Its fluidity made me feel I was floating. Floating amidst the clouds. Wore it once, on my graduation day.

Then, the dark green dress with golden brushstrokes was stored, hanged in my family's lent bedroom. The closet decorated with deep wine red velvet. Till it was no more.

Till this day, I miss my graduation dress. Never knew where it went. It was long and from a colour not to be missed, if misplaced. Easily spottable. Easily recognisable. Easily identifiable.

There was only my copy.

Never dared to ask what happened to it. My mom having passed away, it is now too late to ask her what happened to it. Better so, the answer, if I got an answer, might have made me cry.

THE PROCESSION OF LIGHTS

My mother raised me deeply devout to Catholicism.

In Portugal, each village has a patron, protective Saint. The Saints feasts invariably happen during the Summer months.

There is Santo António with its grilled sardines in the stairs of Alfama in Lisbon. My place of birth also has a Feast of Santo António.

I volunteered. We prepared colourful banners and lines hanging in the streets.

Raffles by folding small squares of colourful paper, salivated to hold it closed, and folded in two. Some had numbers corresponding to prices that had been donated by local businesses.

And with each Saint's Feast there is a pilgrimage, a procession.

The Procession has the image of the Saint, sometimes of other Saints also being carried by deacons and members of the clergy, or and believers.

Processions are deeply impressive occasions, if one is prone, given to believe.

I am a believer. I believe in ghosts.

Believe in the afterlife even if I fear to die. I believe souls that have unresolved issues, which were unsettled at the times of their passing away, come back to resolve what is unresolved.

We light candles in processions. We walk to Fátima in pilgrimage. We make sacrifices by not eating.

I began reading tarots amateurly years back. In my tarot cards, an old shaman takes a candle and searches for a good person. The good person is given the candle and searches himself for a good person.

The last years I have not taken part in many processions and pilgrimages. I do make promises often. I will be participating in pilgrimages, walking, and in processions, I trust, in future.

VIOLET

Violet is not purple. Violet is a spectral colour and purple is the result of diverse mismatching of red and blue (or violet) light.

I have had very seldom hematomas. Those that I did have were violet.

In my lent bedroom I had a conch, a spiny dye-murex, which is a source of the purple dye. WE brought it from Algarve one Summer. By placing it against my ear, I could hear the sea waves distinctly.

On the small bedside table there was a lamp with an image of the Virgin Mary of Lourdes. Her robe blue and her headscarf white. The oval image was lined by small conchs. The lamp was at its bottom, directly illuminating when lit the Virgin Mary of Lourdes's face.

GREEN

Greenish woods, trees, leaves. My favourite colour.

YELLOW

When babies are born we give gold: bracelets, rings, necklaces, what our budget allows and what the degree of familiarity demands.

Over the years I gave my daughter the gold I inherited from my mom. Together with the gold she received upon her birth.

All my kitchens have been painted yellow. My eldest uncle's and aunt's kitchen was also yellow. Yellow for me is the colour of sun and warmth, of honey and peaches and mango.

BLACK

Portugal is the country where black is a colour, read the Oporto wine ad in the bus stop.

I was waiting near my house. A familiar face approached and, with his long cape, or long overcoat better, bent over me and tried to kiss me. Like the logo in Sandeman Oporto wine of the Oporto wine as in the bus stop. I hastily run away.

The same familiar someone who later approached me on a train I took, going home from work. To whom I replied in French, when I was approached, *Who do you think you are?*

Elderly women widows often wear black till they die, in Portugal. They crochet seating at their doorsteps.

I have only knew my granny in black.

Coimbra's university togas are black. So is a judge's toga. I am not a black person: I thrive in colour.

GIVING

I promised no longer to give what I cannot miss.

It's a Portuguese fado song that sings *if (she) did not give what (she) misses. 'Se não tivesse dado o que lhe faz falta.'*

Can be my imagination. I do see my life in films, Netflix, Hollywood, Bollywood. Others. In books. In songs. Like they all speak of me. Like I am nude to the world. Like they even know more about me than I know about myself.

I gave often and gave generously. The more I gave, the more I was asked to give. Till I was no longer asked and giving became an obligation, for which I would have negative repercussions if not obliging.

I have learnt my lessons. Hard precious lessons.

Lesson number one is to only help those in actual need.

Lesson number two is to help within the delimitations of my possibilities: if by helping I become homeless, I am not helping myself.

Lesson number three is to respect myself as much as I respect others.

Lesson number four is intimately intertwined with lesson number three, and this is: to care for me and love myself as much as I care for and love others. My self-preservation.

WATER

Can you give me a glass of water? My eldest sister was closer to the tap in the kitchen than I was, given I was across the room, near the door. My back turned to the door. Yet, I was standing and he was seating at the table.

The water of the well is potable: so fresh and really good for you. Take the jug, the blue there and go and get us some water.

Your uncle has had the water of the well tested. It's perfectly drinkable.

One of my punishments was to show me water, placing it within a reaching distance from me, and forbidding me to drink it. I would look at it, but could not touch it.

A way to drink was to water the plants in the garden. I could drink from that water, even if it was running in dirty soil.

Another way to drink was to iron clothes: the iron's steam function needs water in its reservoir. Whilst dispensing the water into the iron, I could surreptitiously drink a few water sips.

Another way still was to handwash clothes in the small tank: before soaping the cloths, I could again surreptitiously drink a few sips.

The secret is to be docile: and then there are ways to deceptively drink some sips of water.

A mug near the window to collect rain water is another possibility: I did it often.

WINE, THE GRAPE VINE

Every Summer, during the hot Summer months, we have the harvest of the grapes and making of wine. Almost all households in the Portuguese countryside make their own wine, for small the harvest may be.

I remember fondly the family, friends, acquaintances, workers that came and help us. And we returning the favour and helping them.

All grape vine harvests commence at the early hours of the dawn. As early as 5ish in the morning.

Invariably there are straw and cloth hats shared and passed around. Children join and play together under the surveillance of an youngster, sometimes I was the youngster.

It was the opportunity to meet the family and friends. Some that we would only see then.

The lunches lasted long, can be abrasive during the midday, high sun hours.

The grapes were collected and brought in large baskets. Then macerated and let it ferment. Sulphur was burnt to frighten the insects.

Burnt sulphur has a very bright yellow flame and a very strong, penetrating, invasive odour.

Grapes are central to my life. Wine is central to my life. Converting water into wine is central to my life.

Make wine is metaphoric for patience: it is a time-consuming, demanding process. The maceration needs to degrade.

Ferment. The remains of the maceration were used to prepare '*água ardente*', literally *fire water*. In an alembic. Distilled and bottle by each family. A family's own make, own brand. To share with those visiting in ulterior occasions.

Portugal's equivalent to Brazil's '*cachaça*' and '*caipirinha*'.

CUTTING

I am dying. I think more than I usually do, now, because of my actual circumstances. Because time presses, I became choosy. Choose my past times, my hobbies, my interests.

Choose the people I want to spend time with. Choose my priorities. Choose the clothes and jewels I prefer to wear.

Very little is left to luck at the moment. I want to devour each second, whilst energising me and resting as much as feasible to recover as much as I can. I am hoping for a miracle. I am aspiring to live longer than predicted.

Circumstantial events demanded I kept a distance. There were tears, anxiety, vexation. Sadness, deep sadness. Anger and annoyance. Sometimes is not possible otherwise, and after a while one does not become habituated by comes to terms with one's circumstances. This happened with me.

I would be exhausted, emotionally worn out. Sleeping in public places or when others conversed so densely that I wan not able to have my say. Was not able to intervene into the constant mesmerizing much of their verbosity.

I can cut. Let go. Hurts me in many ways. Nonetheless, I can let go. Forgiving but not forgetting.

I have not cut with my earlier existence. Did cut with some people and places from my earlier existence.

What is left is tiredness. Often exhaustion. Wary of similar circumstances.

I fear that I become, and will increasingly become, fearsome. I was fearless as a young adult. Now I am different. Much of the fearlessness diluted with time.

I did become more resolute for what I do not fear. Seems a contradiction, but it is not. I stand for my choices. And take responsibility for my deeds.

Why haven't you called? Why haven't you written?

I did call and did write. Just the calls were not answered, nor were the letters and cards.

In my cookies box, with Mont Saint Michel printed in the metal cover, I keep my letters and cards. Of family events, funerals, weddings, Christmas wishes. The family photos.

I keep my breathing slow and low because of my chest pain. I should cut with those insulting me still, I know. If I cut with all I have a reason to cut with, there will not be many left.

I am dying in all likelihood. I convince myself the doctors who made the diagnostic and macabre prediction do not know me enough. It were not my usual treating doctors. *Should I forgive and let it be? Should I turn my back and walk away?* Life is circumstantial.

WHEN I DIE

When I die, in one year from today. Or later, I pray. I want Enrique Iglesias song *Nunca Te Olvidaré* to be played at my funeral. Because 3,000 years can pass and I will never forget (you).

I am afraid of dying. I love life. Do not want to die.

FINALE

Despite all the darkness, I recall so much light and happiness in my life. Have been lucky to know deep love and esteem, from me and towards me.

Have been lucky to travel and enjoy. Have been in places that many only can dream of being in and at.

Like UNESCO patrimony not even in a normal map.

Places to the fortunate few.

Have lived a full, rich and enriching life: I have tried to correct my faults and apologise for my mistakes.

I have tried to live a healthy, sane and just life.

To be kind to persons and animals.

To forgive and understand.

I lived and live with respect.

My abuse was inflicted to me, but I refuse to be an abuser.

Do my utmost best to live within the limits of the law, be it divine or human.

I have been lucky to have been, and be, a spouse, a mom, a daughter, a sister, a sister-in-law, a daughter-in-law, a granddaughter, an aunt, a friend and a lover.

I am lucky.

I love myself to bits: *and every day I repeat to myself, as now here preparing for a restful night, that all in all, I am probably the luckiest and happiest woman on Earth: to survive what I have survived is in itself not only a feat, but a beautiful miracle.*

I am so very fortunate !

Thank you for reading me.

AUTHOR BIOGRAPHY

This is the author's debut as writer. She was born in Portugal and has since long lived in Belgium. She is a wife and mother. This is a completely fictional short story of hope and resilience amidst much darkness in a girl's early infancy and teen years.

She loves travelling and meeting new people.

She studied in US, Portugal, Scotland and Belgium and has an executive MBA in International Management. She started her own company, Roxo BV, last year and is an active freelancer in the life sciences industry.

Printed in the United States
by Baker & Taylor Publisher Services